W9-BEJ-185

THE MAGIC OF TEAMWORK

by L.M. Colozza
illustrated by Soud

HOUGHTON MIFFLIN HARCOURT
School Publishers

Copyright © by Houghton Mifflin Harcourt Publishing Company

All rights reserved. No part of this work may be reproduced or transmitted in any form or by any means, electronic or mechanical, including photocopying or recording, or by any information storage and retrieval system, without the prior written permission of the copyright owner unless such copying is expressly permitted by federal copyright law. Requests for permission to make copies of any part of the work should be addressed to Houghton Mifflin Harcourt School Publishers, Attn: Permissions, 6277 Sea Harbor Drive, Orlando, Florida 32887-6777.

Printed in China

ISBN-10: 0-547-25346-X
ISBN-13: 978-0-547-25346-6

7 8 0940 18 17 16 15 14 13 12
4500368025

If you have received these materials as examination copies free of charge, Houghton Mifflin Harcourt School Publishers retains title to the materials and they may not be resold. Resale of examination copies is strictly prohibited.

Possession of this publication in print format does not entitle users to convert this publication, or any portion of it, into electronic format.

It was the first day of school. Mom pulled out her checklists. "Keisha, you're first," she said. "Do you have everything you need for your first day of middle school?"

Keisha nodded and stepped forward. Mom read from her list. "Backpack?"

"Check," Keisha said, lifting the bag.

"Notebooks and pencils?"

"Check!" Keisha placed the last items in her bag.

Mom smiled, "It looks like you're ready!"

Keisha's school supplies are on the counter.

Darnell's mother checks his supplies.

Next, I stepped forward. Mom began reading my checklist. When she finished, she looked me in the eye and said, "Darnell, have you decided what instrument you want to play in the fourth-grade band?"

"Sax," I replied, as I began playing my imaginary saxophone.

"Well, team," Mom announced. "It looks like we're ready for the day."

"Not yet," I said. "Today is your first day back to work, Mom. Where is *your* checklist?"

"Here it is," Mom said. "My checklist is in the new briefcase your father gave me."

Darnell's mother has a new briefcase.

The family is getting ready to leave in the morning.

My little brother, Malik, and I quickly had breakfast. Keisha left for school.

"You're taking the boys to school, right?" Mom asked Dad.

He nodded. "I know the plan. This family is a well-oiled machine," he said. "We always run smoothly."

Little did he know that something unusual was going to happen.

After a few weeks, we found that balancing the combination of school and work schedules was turning out to be very hard.

When Mom came home late one evening, she followed the blaring music to my sister's door. "Turn off that racket," she ordered. "Is your homework done?"

"Not yet," Keisha answered.

Mom called up to Malik, "Did you have your bath?"

"Not yet," he answered.

Our routine was definitely off schedule.

That night a storm woke me up. Looking outside, I saw a dog staring at me in the yard. Suddenly, lightning flashed, and it was gone. *I must be dreaming*, I thought.

The next morning, I came downstairs, got my lunch money, and said to Mom, "I have a field trip today. Did you sign my permission slip?"

"What slip?" she asked.

I pointed at the papers on the table.

Darnell's mother is looking for the permission slip.

Mom quickly handed me the signed slip as Keisha stomped by with her favorite shirt, which hadn't been washed. When Dad walked in to the kitchen, he grumbled, "There's no coffee in the pot."

Mom sunk into a chair and sighed. "I suggest we have a family meeting tonight. We need a new plan."

Darnell's Mom wants to have a family meeting.

CHART

MOM   LAUNDRY
DAD   BREAKFAST
KEISHA   LUNCHES
DARNELL   DINNER
MALIK   PAPER WORK
             CLEANING
             FEEDING
             THE CAT

Darnell's dad explains the chore chart.

That night, we all sat at the kitchen table. Dad hung a chart on the fridge and said, "We need a strong effort to get things running smoothly again."

Dad wrote our names and a list of jobs on the chart. "Mom already does laundry on Saturday, so I'll do laundry on Wednesday."

"I'll make extra meals to reheat for dinner during the week," Mom continued.

Darnell dries off the large dog.

"I'll make our lunches the night before," Keisha volunteered.

"Will this really work?" I asked.

Suddenly, a loud clap of thunder shook the house. I heard a sound at the back door and opened it, thinking it was our cat. A yellow dog ran inside and shook the rain from his shaggy fur. I dried him off with a towel.

"You can't keep the dog," my parents said.

"But," I said, "He doesn't have a collar."

The dog barked, pointing toward the door. I opened it, and our cat, Whiskers, came running in. Malik laughed, "It's raining cats and dogs!"

The dog's timing had been good—that was a little strange. I pointed at the chart. "I'll clear the table and take care of the dog."

The cat runs inside when Darnell opens the door.

"The dog can stay, but only until we find its owners," Mom said.

Thunder boomed overhead. "Let's call him Boomer," Malik suggested.

Right away, there was something special about Boomer. The next morning, he stood by each of our beds and barked until we got up. Then Boomer stood by the table and barked. Malik set the table.

Boomer barks to get the boys out of bed.

The kitchen is ready for the family to start the morning.

We began to realize that Boomer was no ordinary dog. He was focused on keeping each of us on track. Every day, Boomer made sure Keisha, Malik, and I did our chores.

The next week, Boomer nudged us to the chart instead. Before long, with teamwork and a little help from a dog, our family was once again working like a well-oiled machine.

Boomer is gone.

One evening, another thunderstorm rolled in. Our family was at the table, while Whiskers and Boomer were curled up on the kitchen rug. A clap of thunder shook the house. In a flash, Boomer was gone.

We don't know where he came from or where he went. But I know that if things stop running smoothly again, Boomer will be back.

Responding

✓ **TARGET SKILL** **Theme** What do the characters' actions suggest about the theme of the story? Copy and complete the chart below.

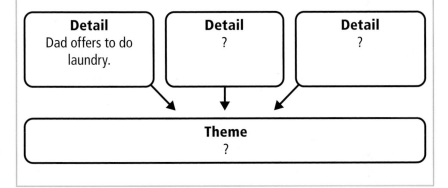

Detail
Dad offers to do laundry.

Detail
?

Detail
?

Theme
?

Write About It

Text to Text Think about another book you have read in which the main characters work together to solve a problem. Write a paragraph comparing and contrasting this problem with the problem in *The Magic of Teamwork*.

✔ TARGET VOCABULARY

appreciate	introduce
blaring	nocturnal
combination	promptly
effort	racket
feats	suggest

✔ **TARGET SKILL** **Theme** Understand character's qualities, motives, and actions to recognize the theme of the story.

✔ **TARGET STRATEGY** **Summarize** Briefly tell the important parts of the text in your own words.

GENRE A **fantasy** is a story with details that could not happen but seem real.